# A Skipping Day

**Adapted by Andrea Posner-Sanchez**

Story concept by Tea Orsi

**Illustrated by Stefania Fiorillo,**
**Raffaella Seccia, and Gianluca Barone**

 **A GOLDEN BOOK • NEW YORK**

randomhouse.com/kids     ISBN: 978-0-7364-3029-6     Printed in the United States of America

10  9  8  7  6  5  4

It's a nice day on Shipwreck Beach. Jake and his crew are playing with a jump rope.

"Yay hey! This jump rope is fun!" Izzy says.

"It's awesome!" Jake agrees.

Skully flutters this way and that way, happily
flying under the rope when he gets a chance.

Jake, Izzy, and Skully don't know it, but Captain Hook is spying on them with his spyglass.

"Those puny pirates are having fun with that jumpy thing," says Hook. "I want to have fun, too!"

"I must have that jumpy thing," Captain Hook
tells his first mate, Mr. Smee. "Get me that treasure!"
Mr. Smee salutes Hook and says, "Yes, Cap'n!"

Meanwhile, back on the beach, the pirate crew is ready for a healthy snack.

"It's smoothie time, mateys!" announces Cubby.

"Thanks, Cubby," says Izzy. "All that jumping has made me thirsty."

"Those look great, Cubby!" says Jake.
Jake puts the jump rope on the sand. After he and his friends drink their smoothies, they will jump some more.

Jake, Izzy, and Skully head over to Cubby.
"Crackers! I love smoothies!" says Skully.

As the pirates enjoy their drinks, Captain Hook and Smee sneak onto the beach. "The jumpy thing is mine, Smee!" Hook declares.

Skully spots the scoundrels. "It's
Captain Hook!" he cries.
   Jake turns just in time to see Hook
and Smee running away.

"Hey! He stole our jump rope!"
Izzy says as Captain Hook and
Smee head into Tiki Tree Forest.
"Yo ho! Let's get our treasure
back!" declares Jake.

The pirate crew rushes to catch up with Hook and Smee. Unfortunately, a river stops them in their tracks.

"Aw, coconuts! How did Hook and Smee get to the other side of this river?" Cubby asks.

Izzy thinks for a moment. Then she comes up with a solution. "We'll jump on the stones to cross the river," she says. Jake thinks it's a great idea. "Yo ho! Way to go!"

"Let's do it on the count of three," says Izzy.
"One, two, three!"

Jake, Izzy, and Cubby jump on the rocks and cross the river. Skully cheers them on. "Crackers! You're doing it!" calls the parrot.

Everyone is having fun. "I love jumping!" exclaims Cubby.

When they reach the other side of the
river, Jake and his crew quickly catch up to
Captain Hook and Mr. Smee.

"Please give us back our jump rope, Captain Hook!" cries Jake.

"Never!" Captain Hook says. "It's my turn to have fun!"

Hook is all set to finally play with the jump rope.
Izzy notices that the rope is tangled around his feet.
"Watch out, Hook!" Izzy warns.

But Captain Hook doesn't listen.
He falls to the ground, all tied up.
"Smee!" Hook cries. "Save meee!"

Izzy and Jake rush over to help. In no time, the
friends free Captain Hook from the jump rope.

"Barnacles! That jumpy thing is broken," Captain Hook declares. "I don't want it anymore."

"It's not broken," Jake says, smiling.

"We'll teach you how to use it," Izzy adds.

The jolly buccaneers show Captain Hook and Smee what to do. Before long, they're all jumping—and having fun!

"I'm jumping, Smee! I'm jumping!" shouts Hook happily.

"Well done, Cap'n," says Smee.